A Puppy Called Disaster

Look for all
the books in the

PET RESCUE CLUB
series

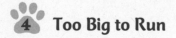

A Puppy Called Disaster

by Rose Hapkins

illustrated by Dana Regan

Cover Illustration by Steve James

Studio Fun International
An imprint of Printers Row Publishing Group
10350 Barnes Canyon Road, Suite 100, San Diego, CA 92121
www.studiofun.com

Printers Row Publishing Group is a division of Readerlink Distribution Services, LLC.
Studio Fun International is a registered trademark of Readerlink Distribution Services, LLC.

All notations of errors or omissions should be addressed to
Studio Fun International, Editorial Department, at the above address.

ISBN: 978-0-7944-4006-0
Manufactured, printed, and assembled in China.
20 19 18 17 16   1 2 3 4 5

***The American Society for the Prevention of Cruelty to Animals (ASPCA®)
will receive a minimum guarantee from Studio Fun International, Inc. of
$25,000 for the sale of ASPCA® products through December 2017.**

Comments? Questions? Call us at: 1-888-217-3346

Library of Congress Cataloging-in-Publication Data

Hapkins, Rose. Reagan, Dana, illustrator.
A Puppy Called Disaster / by Rose Hapkins ; illustrated by Dana Reagan.
White Plains, New York: Studio Fun Books, [2016].
Series: Pet Rescue Club ; 5 | "ASPCA Kids."
Summary: When a tornado strikes, the Third Street Pet Shelter overflows with animals
separated from their owners, so Janey and her friends help take care of them.
LCCN 2016011146 | ISBN 9780794438098 (paperback) | ISBN 9780794438548 (e-book)
ISBN 9780794440060 (paperback)
[CYAC: Tornadoes—Fiction. | Pets—Fiction. | Petadoption—Fiction.
Animal shelters—Fiction. | Clubs—Fiction.]
BISAC: JUVENILE FICTION / Animals / Pets. | JUVENILE FICTION / Social Issues
General (see also headings under Family). | JUVENILE FICTION / Readers / Chapter Books.
Classification: LCC PZ7.1.H3645 Pup 2016 | DDC [Fic]—dc23
LC record available at https://lccn.loc.gov/2016011146

To my new friend Sue,
who came through.

—R. H.

Storm Warning

"Are you going to eat that?" Zach Goldman reached toward the large, plastic-wrapped cookie in Janey Whitfield's lunch box. It was lunchtime at school, and Zach and Janey and their friends Lolli Simpson and Adam Santos—the members of the Pet Rescue Club—were having a meeting.

The four schoolmates had formed the club after helping to rescue a neglected dog named Truman. After helping Truman find a home with their homeroom teacher, Ms. Tanaka, they'd helped other animals. Now they were itching for a new case.

"Hands off, Zach," said Janey. She playfully swatted Zach's hand away. Then she took the cookie from its plastic wrap and broke it into quarters. "Lolli, do you want a piece of my Choco-Tornado-Treat?"

Lolli patted her stomach. Black, curly hair tumbled over her face. "Thanks, but I'm full," she said.

"Besides, you know her food is all natural, all the time," said Zach. Lolli's mother and father never gave Lolli any store-bought treats. They called themselves back-to-the-land hippies.

Janey eyed the remains of Lolli's lunch—brown rice with brown beans and brown tofu with soy sauce. It looked very unappealing.

"More for me," said Zach. With three older brothers, he was in the habit of eating as much as he could as fast as he could. He grabbed Lolli's piece of Choco-Tornado-Treat and ate it in one bite.

Adam adjusted his glasses on his nose, and then opened his mouth to snap up the bite of cookie Janey tossed to him, as if he were one of the dogs he trained and cared for in his pet-sitting business. Even though Adam was only nine, people all over town paid him to come to their houses to feed and walk their dogs while they were at work or on vacation. "Arf, arf," Adam said, jokingly.

Lolli was the only member of the Pet Rescue Club whose mouth wasn't full of Choco-Tornado-Treat. "Has anybody posted anything new on the blog?" she asked Janey.

Janey's blog had started as a way for kids around town to share photos of their pets. Janey loved animals, but she couldn't have a pet of her own because her father was severely allergic to anything with fur or feathers. She had to make do with seeing pictures of cute animals on the tablet she'd been given for her birthday. Now the blog had another purpose, too. The Pet Rescue Club used the blog to find animals that needed its help.

Janey swallowed. But before she could answer Lolli, the principal's voice came over the public address system. "School will close early. There is a severe weather warning for the area. Students are to board buses or meet their parents outside the school building."

Everyone began to talk at once. "Yay, no school!" said Zach.

"This doesn't seem like a time for jokes," said Janey. All the kids were getting up from their tables at once. A fifth grader pushed Janey as he ran for the door.

The principal's voice came again from the speakers overhead. "Students will exit the cafeteria in an orderly manner, please! Walk, don't run!" Kids kept running. "I said, walk!" squawked the speaker.

"Does the principal have x-ray eyes? It's as if she can see us all the way from the office!" Zach joked. Janey scowled at him. "Oh, laugh a little, Janey," said Zach. Janey smiled, but only a little.

Outside, the members of the Pet Rescue Club boarded the school bus. They lived in different parts of town, but the bus route passed nearby each one's house.

"Look at that sky," Adam said as he took his seat beside Zach. "It's pretty dark and gloomy."

Lolli and Janey took seats side by side. "I hope Roscoe is okay," Lolli said. "He hates storms." Roscoe was the Simpsons' big, lovable dog. Lolli and her parents had found him at the Third Street Animal Shelter a few years earlier. He was a mix of Labrador retriever, rottweiler, and nobody knew what else. Roscoe and Zach's orange tabby cat, Mulberry, were the Pet Rescue Club's official mascots.

"I have an idea," said Adam. "Do you know what an anxiety vest is?" Adam had noticed that many of the dogs he cared for were afraid during storms. Then he had learned about a special vest that wrapped snugly around a dog's body. The vest seemed to make the dogs feel calmer during a thunder and lightning storm.

"My dad heard about those from Zach's mom," said Lolli. Dr. Goldman was a veterinarian with a busy private practice, who also helped take care of the pets at the animal shelter. "We're going to get one for Roscoe soon."

The other kids on the bus were singing at the top of their lungs, as if they were heading home for a school vacation and there was nothing wrong. But there was something wrong. Janey couldn't help thinking about the pets at the Third Street Animal Shelter.

"The pets at the shelter will be scared," said Janey. If she could, she would give all of them lots of hugs. "I wish we could go to the shelter instead of going home."

Just then, lightning flashed. Thunder boomed.

Janey looked out the school bus window at the storm clouds. She saw a big yellow Lab running wild. The dog had a red collar, but it didn't look like the collar had a tag on it. Janey pointed out the dog to the other members of the Pet Rescue Club. "I sure hope that dog is sprinting home to safety," she said.

2

Lights Out!

In the hour after the school bus dropped Janey off at her house, the weather went from bad to worse. The sky grew thick with dark clouds. Rain fell in sheets. Now there was a sudden racket on the roof.

Janey ran to the window and pulled aside the curtain. "Look!" she cried. "It's hailing outside!" Hail was falling so hard and so heavily that Janey could barely see the mailbox at the curb.

"Everybody, let's go downstairs to the basement!" said Janey's mother. Her face was nearly hidden by the stack of blankets she held in her arms.

"Is the storm that serious?" asked Janey, letting the curtain fall shut and joining her parents.

Janey's parents had been watching the channel seven emergency weather broadcast, and now her father clicked off the TV. "There's no need to be alarmed, sweetheart," he said in a calm voice. He put his hand on Janey's shoulder and guided her toward the basement door. "But chief meteorologist Bob Broad says the weather service has increased the tornado alert from a watch to a warning. That means we need to take shelter in the basement right now. Someone may have spotted a funnel cloud, or else a tornado is showing up on the weather service's radar. They predict high winds and thunderstorms with hail."

Janey's mom jutted her chin toward the window. "Well, he's absolutely right about the hail," she said. "We'll be safer in the basement."

Janey followed her parents downstairs.

The Whitfields' basement was tidy, but unfinished. It didn't have a playroom or family room. It was mostly a big, empty space, one you didn't want to spend a lot of time in. There was a row of shelves along one wall, where her parents had stocked emergency food, water jugs, flashlights, extra batteries, and even some games.

"The Red Cross gave an emergency preparedness course that most of the community took last spring," Janey's mother explained as they went down the stairs. "We're all set, and our neighbors should be, too."

Janey's father set up a folding table and chairs. "We can play board games," he said. "And look! Snacks!" He put out a dish of salted peanuts and chocolate chips. "How about our old friend, Animal Baby Bingo?"

Animal Baby Bingo had been a birthday present when Janey was little. It was still one of her favorite games, because the game pieces and bingo boards were covered with pictures of animals. Janey agreed to play, even though she really wasn't in the mood for games, not even ones with adorable baby animals. She could hear the wind whipping around and the hailstones pounding outside, even way down here in the basement.

Janey's mother turned on a standing lamp beside the table, and set up the bingo game. "See, love? Nice and cozy!" she said, giving Janey's arm a squeeze. "We are snug as three bugs in a rug down here."

Janey tried to concentrate on Animal Baby Bingo. But her mind wandered. She worried about her friends and their pets. Were Truman and Ms. Tanaka together and safe? What was happening beyond the town limits? What about Roscoe, and Lolli's goats and sheep? What about Mrs. Jamison and her pony, Lola, that the Pet Rescue Club helped her to adopt? And she was still thinking about the shelter. Was Kitty, who worked at

the shelter, okay? And were all the pets there safe, too? Looking at all these animal game pieces wasn't helping.

Janey and her parents played a few rounds of bingo, and Janey almost started to forget about the reason they were playing games downstairs in their drab basement.

"Bingo!" cried Mr. Whitfield. In his excitement, he hit the dish of snacks with his elbow. Peanuts and chocolate chips went flying!

Just then, there was a deafening roar.

The lights went out.

Janey's heart pounded and she threw her arms over her head. "Mom!" she yelled. "Dad!"

"Right here, sweetheart!" her father yelled. She could hardly hear his voice over the long, loud, rumbling noise that filled her ears. Janey felt a firm hand on her arm. She grabbed it and held on tight. Bangs and cracks and creaks came from over their heads. Janey held her breath and squeezed her eyes shut.

"Hang in there, Janey," her father shouted over the awful racket. "It'll be over soon!"

Emergency
at the Shelter

Mr. Whitfield was right. The tornado was over almost as soon as it began. Janey's mother set a battery-powered emergency lantern on the table and turned it on. Then she put her arms around Janey and rocked her back and forth. When they were sure the storm had really passed and the danger was really over, they went upstairs and looked around.

"Everything looks good inside," said Mrs. Whitfield after a quick check of all the rooms. Then they went outside.

"Only a few shingles blew off the roof," Janey's father said. They stood in front of the house, blinking in the sudden sunshine. The sky was clear. It looked as if the tornado had blown away all the dark clouds.

Janey looked around in wonder. Everything seemed so quiet, now. The yard was a mess of branches. "We'll have to play the world's biggest game of pick-up sticks," she said.

Her mother nodded. "But this is no game, love," she said. "Let's go and see how our friends and neighbors have weathered the storm."

Janey picked her way carefully through the yard and out onto the street, staying close to her parents. They walked past garbage cans rolling on their sides in the street.

They stepped around a heavy iron lawn chair lying on its back with its legs in the air. Janey gasped when she saw that a big tree limb had crashed onto the roof of a car parked on the corner.

Doors opened up and down the street as neighbors came out of their houses to see what had happened. Mrs. Peacham, three houses down, stepped onto her porch. Her little Chihuahua, Bimminy, shivered in her arms.

"Are you all right?" Janey's dad asked Mrs. Peacham. She nodded her head.

"Is Bimminy okay?" Janey asked.

"Poor thing, she cried and cried," said Mrs. Peacham. "But she's all right now, aren't you, Bimminy," she said, rubbing noses with her pet. Bimminy gave a happy little yip-yip.

Mrs. Peacham looked around. "My lawn chair is gone," she said, bewildered.

Janey's mom pointed back down the street. "There it is," she said. "It flew a long way." Everyone on the street began to walk around and explore. Every so often, someone would cry out, "I found it!" That meant they had located something of theirs that had been tossed around by the tornado.

Janey and her parents helped their neighbors move things back to their homes for a while. But then she wanted to go and check on the animals at the shelter. "Please, Mom?" she begged.

"I'm afraid it's not possible right now," Janey's mother said. "You can see that our street is blocked by fallen trees. That means lots of other roads are blocked, too. Power lines are probably down all over town. Even if we were willing to let you walk to Third Street, it's better that we stay out of the utility workers' way right now. It will just be safer for you and for them."

"Maybe tomorrow," said Janey's father.

....

It was a long night. Her house still didn't have any electricity. So, Janey played her favorite game, Puppy Playtime, on her laptop. When the batteries ran out, she read a good book called *Puppies in Paradise* by the light of the emergency lantern. She wished she could talk to her friends, but there was no landline or cell phone service. Finally, she fell asleep and dreamed of puppies crying and crying.

"Time to go to the shelter!" Janey said first thing the next morning, even though the electricity still wasn't back on. But it was noon by the time the area was cleared of debris and Janey was allowed to go. Her mother walked with her. "Why does everything look so different?" Janey wondered as they made their way to Third Street. Even the light outside seemed to have changed.

"It does look different," her mother agreed. "Look! That big maple tree split and fell." She pointed to several large chunks of tree trunk. Workers had cut up the fallen tree in order to make Third Street passable. "It's amazing how much difference one tree makes," she said.

After what felt like a long time, they arrived at the Third Street Animal Shelter.

"Kitty, we're here!" called Janey. She had to shout to be heard above the noise of barking, yipping, howling, and meowing. The shelter was normally a bit on the noisy side. But the pets were so loved and so well cared for during their stay that it sounded like pets having fun at their version of school recess. Today, though, the pets sounded more stressed.

"Boy, am I glad to see you!" said Kitty. Janey's favorite pet shelter worker was flushed. Her hair was falling out of her usually neat and bouncy blond ponytail.

"I bet you could use a hand," Mrs. Whitfield said.

"I could use as many hands as I can get," Kitty said.

Janey hadn't expected to see so many animals at the pet shelter. "Why is it so crowded here today?" she asked.

"As you may have heard, other parts of town were hit harder than our neighborhood," Kitty explained. "A lot of folks had to evacuate their houses and go to the evacuation center at the high school." Kitty jabbed a thumb in the direction of the high school. "The evacuation center doesn't allow pets," she added.

"What?" Janey was outraged. Of all the times that pets and their people needed to be together, it was during a disaster, she thought. "Why not?" she said, peeking into the dog room as she spoke. Right away, she spotted the big yellow Lab with the red collar she'd seen from the bus yesterday. She had hoped that dog was dashing home. But at least he was safe here, and not still running loose.

"The main reason is that local and state safety regulations don't allow it," said Kitty. She saw the shocked look on Janey's face. "They do have their reasons," Kitty explained. "One is that pets can panic in unusual, stressful situations and they might cause problems if surrounded by tons of strangers."

"And, as we know all too well, some people, like your father, have allergies," Janey's mother added.

Kitty pointed to a thin scar on her wrist. "See that? Scared and stressed animals can be more likely to bite or scratch their owners, other people, or other pets," Kitty said. "I got this when I was taking an old cat from the home where she'd always lived. Her person had to move to an assisted-living facility, and he couldn't keep his cat." Kitty shook her head. "That poor cat was very upset. I didn't take the scratch personally."

"Also, I imagine it's just plain hard to deal with poop patrol when you're stuck inside a high school gym," said Mrs. Whitfield. "I guess we have to think of it as a people shelter, not a pet shelter."

"It's a good thing we have both kinds," said Kitty.

Janey's mother looked at her watch. "I'd like to go and check on some more neighbors now," she said to Janey. "You'll be all right here?" she asked.

"There's no place I'd rather be!" Janey said.

Mrs. Whitfield left, and Kitty put her hands on her hips and looked around. "I've got my hands full, that's for sure," she said. "Some of these dogs and cats have been dropped here by their owners. Others have been separated from their people and found by emergency responders. I'm glad you're here to help, Janey. Thanks for coming!"

Just then, the door burst open. In came Lolli Simpson.

"Lolli!" said Janey, glad to see her best friend. "How is everything out at the farm?"

"Luckily, the tornado didn't hit us out there, but the wind was loud," said Lolli. "Roscoe was scared. I thought of the pets here, and my mom agreed to drop me off so

I could check on them."

Then Dr. Goldman strode in, carrying her medical bag. Close behind her was Zach.

"Hello, everybody," said the veterinarian. "Zach and I thought you could use some help today," she said to Kitty.

"I sure can!" Kitty said.

"How's Mulberry?" Lolli wondered.

"That cat slept through the whole thing," said Zach. "Can you believe it? Didn't even budge when a big branch came crashing down on the garage roof!"

"Wow! It's too bad Roscoe isn't as mellow as that in a storm," said Lolli. "He was shivering and whimpering. We are definitely going to get him an anxiety vest soon!"

Adam Santos was the next one through

the door. Every member of the Pet Rescue Club had had the same idea. This was their new case—not just one animal in need, but a whole bunch of them!

4

Little Lost Puppy

The Santos family had fared the worst of Janey's friends. Adam explained that the roof of the house they rented was damaged when a tree fell, so he and his family had to evacuate to the emergency shelter. Adam described the shelter at the high school. Rows of cots were set up in the cafeteria and the gym. "I guess it's sort of like a summer camp," Adam said. "Only not."

"What about your house?" asked Lolli.

"At night, you can see real stars in the sky instead of the glow-in-the dark stars on my ceiling," said Adam. "There's a big hole right over my bed!"

"Cool!" said Zach.

"Not cool," said Dr. Goldman. "I'm sorry, Adam. Please ask your parents to let me know if there's anything I can do to help."

"Thanks," said Adam. "I'll let them know. But right now, I'm really wanting to help out this man I talked to this morning at the emergency shelter."

Adam told them that the man had said, "'I don't care if I lose my house. My car. It's just stuff. But my dog, Jojo, is missing! I have to find him. I'm lost without him.'"

Adam adjusted his glasses on his nose. "You should have seen the sad look on this guy's face," he said.

Janey could imagine it. Even though she didn't have any pets of her own, she just knew how horrible she would feel if she had one who went missing. "We have to help him find Jojo!" she cried.

"You kids better leave that to the professionals," said a man walking in the door of the shelter. He was wearing the bright orange vest that all the emergency responders had put on.

"Mr. Petersen!" exclaimed Kitty. "You're back again so soon?"

"Yep," he said, with a grim smile. "And, look who I found this time." Mr. Petersen opened his coat. Tucked inside was a wet, shivering puppy.

"Oh, so cute!" squealed Lolli.

Janey was practically breathless. The puppy titled his little head and looked at everyone with sad, dark eyes that stared out from his brown-and-white face. He sniffed the air with his big, dark, button of a nose and gave out a tired, little howl. It was as if the most adorable baby from Animal Baby Bingo had come to life.

"Breathe, Janey," said Zach.

Mr. Petersen explained that as terrible as it was to find a puppy or any pet that has been separated from its family in an emergency situation, in a way he's glad when he does. "It means that people followed the directions to evacuate their homes." He scratched his head, "Some folks refuse to follow evacuation procedures if they can't take their pets with them to an emergency shelter." It was still sad, though, to find pets all alone in an empty house or wandering the streets, like this little, wet puppy. The animals were scared and sad, sometimes injured, and usually very hungry and thirsty.

Dr. Goldman put out her hands to take the puppy from Mr. Petersen. "He looks to be somewhere around three to four months old," she said. "And I think he's got some beagle in him." She checked the puppy all over. Then, she rubbed him dry with a towel that Kitty provided, using brisk but gentle movements.

"This little guy needs to get his blood circulating again," the veterinarian said. "He'll be okay, but someone needs to hold him and keep him warm." Dr. Goldman smiled at Janey. "You think you can handle a job like that, Janey?" she said.

Janey let out the breath she'd been holding. "Oh, yes," she said, reaching out her hands to take the tiny puppy. There was nothing in the world she would rather do.

Kitty pointed at the door to the dog room. "Meanwhile, we've got lots of other dogs. Could someone clean out the cages in there?" she said.

"Not me," Janey said with a smile. "I already have an important job."

"Don't look at me," said Mr. Petersen, laughing.

"Oh, sure," Zach teased. "Let us do all the dirty work."

Zach rolled his eyes, but he knew Janey wouldn't budge from the chair where she sat with the puppy in her arms. The other members of the club indulged her, too. After all, Lolli had Roscoe, and Zach had Mulberry, and Adam had his successful pet sitting business. They all knew that Janey was the one who needed to cuddle the little puppy almost as much as the tiny pup needed cuddling from her.

Soon, the puppy was yipping happily and licking Janey's face. A few minutes later, he fell fast asleep in her lap, with his head in the crook of her elbow.

Dr. Goldman squeezed Janey's shoulder. "That little guy seems much improved, thanks to you," she said.

Janey smiled. "Prodigious!" she said. Janey loved to find special words to use, and prodigious was just the right one to describe the puppy's quick recovery. It certainly seemed wonderful, remarkable, and marvelous to Janey. "I've thought of the perfect name for him," she said.

"I'll call him Disaster. Dizzy, for short."

"Well, I'd best be on my way," said Mr. Petersen, putting on his baseball cap. "Duty calls."

"Where are you off to now?" asked Dr. Goldman.

"An elderly couple out on River Road has no power or water, and it's getting colder," Mr. Petersen said. "They won't leave their house even though there's water hip-deep in the basement. Mr. and Mrs. Witherspoon won't go to the high school and get the food and warmth they need because they don't know what to do with their old dog, Rizzo," he explained.

Kitty pulled on her lip. "I wish we could offer to take care of Rizzo, but we're at full capacity," she said. She glanced over her shoulder at the storage cupboards. "We're also starting to run low on food and supplies because we didn't expect to take in so many pets," she added. "If only we had more room. . . ."

Janey straightened in her chair. The puppy in her arms woke up and blinked. "I have an idea!" Janey said. "And it's totally prodigious!"

Janey's Prodigious Idea

"We could set up an emergency pet shelter!" said Janey. "The pets would have a safe place to be until everything got back to normal. I bet that would make people feel better about getting themselves to safe places, too." Janey turned to Mr. Petersen. "If we could tell Mr. and Mrs. Witherspoon that Rizzo would be safe, do you think they would leave their house and go to the emergency shelter at the high school?"

"I bet they would!" he said. "I think you are on to something, young lady!"

"But where could we open an emergency pet shelter?" Lolli wondered out loud. She, Zach, and Adam had finished cleaning out some of the cages.

"And how would it run?" asked Adam.

"And who would run it?" Zach chimed in with the next question. But he grinned when he said it, because he already knew the answer. "I know, I know," he said. "This is definitely a job for the Pet Rescue Club!"

"Is there a way we can get more food for the pets?" asked Lolli, tugging worriedly on a coil of her hair.

"And what about all the missing pets, like little Dizzy, here," said Janey, rubbing her cheek against the puppy's soft fur. "Can we help find them?"

"Maybe we can use Janey's blog to reunite people with their pets!" said Lolli.

"Whoa, kids," Dr. Goldman finally interrupted, holding up a hand. "We have a saying in veterinary school: one step at a time!"

Zach rolled his eyes. "Mom," he said, "that's not a saying from vet school!"

"It's good, all-purpose advice," said Dr. Goldman, smiling. "Now, what do you need to do first?"

"The first thing we need to do is find a place," said Adam. "It needs to be plenty big, so there's an area where each pet can have its own space. But it also has to have room enough for friendly pets to play together."

Adam knew a lot about caring for and keeping pets happy.

"I wish we had room at our farm to take in a lot more pets," said Lolli. But with Roscoe, two pet goats, a sheep, and a flock of chickens, they didn't have much room to spare.

That got Janey thinking, though. The tornado had gone straight through town. It had just skirted the outlying farmland where Lolli lived. The farms and homes out there were not badly damaged at all. Lola, the pony the Pet Rescue Club had helped, lived on a horse farm just outside of town. Maybe Lola's new owner, Mrs. Jamison, could help the town's pets by letting the Pet Rescue Club set up an emergency animal shelter there!

Janey could hardly get the words out her mouth quickly enough, she was so excited by the idea.

"That's good thinking, Janey," said Kitty, tucking a lock of hair behind her ear that had escaped her ponytail. "But we have no way to call her, since phone service is still out."

"I can take you there in my truck," said Mr. Petersen. "My big rig gets around better than smaller cars." He settled his baseball cap on his head. "Like I said, duty calls. Let's go!"

Since there was no way to contact the other parents quickly, Dr. Goldman gave Janey, Lolli, Adam, and Zach permission to go to Mrs. Jamison's horse farm with Mr. Petersen. "I know all your parents well, and I'm sure they'll be on board with the idea," she said. They all piled into Mr. Petersen's truck. Fifteen minutes later, Mr. Petersen was pulling up in front of Mrs. Jamison's big red barn. She came out of her house and greeted them warmly.

"It's always good to see my friends from the Pet Rescue Club," she said. "What brings you out my way? I understand the damage in town is quite severe."

Janey tapped her foot impatiently as Mr. Petersen described the scene in town, the downed trees and power lines. "As tornados go, it wasn't a big one, but it still managed to cause some damage," he said.

"My goodness," said Mrs. Jamison. "How awful! I remember when I was a little girl, there was a terrible storm. My cat Meow-Meow went missing for about two weeks. We were worried sick! I wandered around calling her name, Meow-Meow here and Meow-Meow there! Eventually she did come back."

"That's the kind of happy ending I like to hear," said Mr. Petersen.

Janey couldn't take it anymore. "I'm glad Meow-Meow came back," she said. "And I don't mean to interrupt. But that's kind of why we're here, Mrs. Jamison."

"Oh?" Mrs. Jamison raised an eyebrow.

"The Third Street Animal Shelter is totally full," Adam explained. He glanced at Mrs. Jamison's barn.

"And there are lots of pets who were separated from their people during the storm," said Lolli. She, too, looked at the big red barn.

"Just like you and Meow-Meow," said Zach, sizing up the barn as he spoke.

Janey took a deep breath. "We were hoping that you would let us set up a temporary pet shelter here in your barn," she said all in a rush. It made her a little bit nervous to ask such an important question.

Janey need not have been so nervous.

Mrs. Jamison smiled warmly. "After all you kids have done? I'd be happy to help in any way I can," she said.

"Prodigious!" said Janey.

"Just so you know, though, the power is out here, too," said Mrs. Jamison. "But if it's room you need, the barn's got plenty. Red and Lola will be glad of the company."

Red was a retired racehorse that Mrs. Jamison had taken in. Lola the pony was Red's long-lost companion. The Pet Rescue Club had helped reunite the old friends, and that's when Mrs. Jamison had decided to adopt Lola, too.

"And there's a wood stove in there," Mrs. Jamison went on. "The barn will be nice and warm for the dogs and cats."

"And turtles," said Zach.

Adam gave Zach a funny look.

"You never know," said Zach with a shrug. "There might be turtles."

Mrs. Jamison opened her arms wide. "It'll be fun, and a bit wild. It'll be like Noah's ark, or the circus! I officially agree to open my barn to all the pets in need," she said. "Even turtles."

Everyone laughed.

A thoughtful look crossed Mrs. Jamison's face. "But I have one condition," she said.

"What's that?" asked Lolli. She and Janey

exchanged a worried look. What if Mrs. Jamison wanted money, or something else they didn't have?

"You kids and at least one adult must be here at all times to take care of the animals," said Mrs. Jamison. "I certainly can't handle running a temporary pet shelter myself."

Janey breathed a sigh of relief. "The Pet Rescue Club will take care of everything," Janey promised. "Don't worry about a thing."

Knocking
on Doors

A half hour later, Janey, Lolli, Zach, and Adam were back at the Third Street Animal Shelter. Janey had gone straight to check on Dizzy, and had found him snoozing comfortably in a small crate. She wanted nothing more than to pick up Dizzy and hold him, but there was work to be done.

Kitty was running around frazzled. In the short time they'd been gone, first to Mrs. Jamison's, and then to get permission from their parents to stay on the horse farm overnight, several more animals had come in to the shelter. There just wasn't space for them. "The dog room's full of dogs," Kitty said. "The cat room's full of cats. Even the Meet-and-Greet room is full of animals, and some of them aren't on their best behavior at the moment." She shook her head. Her ponytail drooped. "I don't blame them. These poor pets have been through a lot! I'm trying to follow quarantine protocol, but I can't keep up with the demand."

Janey quickly shared the good news: The Pet Rescue Club had found a place to set up a temporary emergency pet shelter.

"We'll call it the Big Red Pet Shelter," said Lolli.

Kitty was so relieved that she dropped into a chair and blew back a lock of blond hair that had fallen onto her face.

"That's fantastic," Kitty said, beaming. "And not a minute too soon!"

The four friends got busy making a list of everything in the shelter—they would need to get everything they saw for the Big Red Pet Shelter.

"We need animal crates . . . and food . . . and bedding . . . " said Janey, reading off the list they had made. She made a doodle next to each item.

Zach tossed a rubber ball pet toy in the air and caught it. "And we need all of it in a hurry," said Zach. "Why are you wasting time prettying up the list?"

Janey scowled at Zach. "Doodling helps me think," she said. Janey hadn't been sure about Zach joining the Pet Rescue Club at first. He was always joking around, even when they had serious things to do. But he was a whiz with computers, and he had helped a lot with setting up and managing the blog. And, she had to admit, he'd worked really hard to solve the problem of Hall Cat, a senior, indoor cat whose people kept trying to turn into an outdoor cat. Hall Cat had finally been adopted, thanks to the Pet Rescue Club, by the grandmother of a schoolmate.

"If only we could plug in your laptop," Zach said, tossing the ball between his hands. "Everything would go faster with a keyboard. We could post a message on the blog and also send out e-mails to local businesses, asking for donations. We could get things done."

"If we had power, we wouldn't have a lot of these problems to begin with!" said Janey. She eyed Zach's rubber ball. "Pet toys," she said, adding another important item to the growing list of things they needed.

"How are we going to get all this stuff?" asked Lolli.

Zach sighed. "With no Internet, I guess we'll have to do things the old-fashioned way," he said.

Just then, the door opened.

"Hi, Mrs. Simpson!" said Janey. Lolli's mother walked in, brushing some pieces of hay from her coat sleeves. "Ready to head back to the farm, Lolli?" she asked.

"Well, do you have time to help us with something, Mom?" Lolli asked her mother.

Mrs. Simpson checked her watch. "Sure! My errands took less time than I expected, and the roads have mostly been cleared. What did you have in mind?"

Lolli smiled at her friends. "A little old-fashioned knocking on doors."

....

They started at the local hardware store. Ms. Winkins gladly lent them several folding crates. "Keep those crates for as long as you need them," she said. "I stocked way too many of them back when the potbellied pig craze was in full swing. I haven't sold any in ages."

Then they stopped at the grocery store,

where they were given several cases of canned dog and cat food, some bags of dry food, kitty litter, and cat litter boxes. After that, they visited the butcher, who gave them a sack of bones.

At each business, one of the members of the Pet Rescue Club explained their urgent mission. "We are setting up an emergency pet shelter for pets displaced by the tornado. Will you help us help the pets? We are asking for donations of food, crates, toys, and other supplies."

"How about blankets?" asked Mr. Teaberry at the furniture shop. "I have a pile of moving blankets out back. You're welcome to those, if they'd be useful."

"Prodigious!" said Janey. "Thank you!"

While Janey and Lolli visited businesses, accompanied by Mrs. Simpson, Adam and Zach and Zach's mother went from house to house, knocking on doors and asking for small donations.

People were eager and happy to help in any way they could. Soon the Pet Rescue Club had collected plenty of supplies. It was heartwarming to find out that everyone was more than willing to help pets—and their people—in need.

The kids brought all the generous donations to the Third Street shelter. But now they had another problem. "How are we going to get all this stuff from here to Mrs. Jamison's place?" asked Adam, looking at the boxes and bags and crates piled high by the shelter

door. "We'll have to ask for more help."

"Ask, and you shall receive!" said Mr. Petersen. He'd come back to the shelter with a pet corn snake in a shoebox labeled Mango. "I have to head out that way, and would be glad to drop off the supplies." He took off his baseball cap and scratched his head. "In fact, why don't I make a couple of trips?" he suggested. "I'll deliver all the animals, too. We'll call my truck the official Pet Emergency Transport System."

"PETS!" said Adam, after a moment's thought.

Mr. Petersen winked.

It did take several trips. With Kitty and Dr. Goldman's help, the Pet Rescue Club loaded the PETS with seven cats, nine dogs, two guinea pigs, one ferret, four chickens, one turtle, and Mango the snake. By early evening, all the pets had been delivered to the Big Red Pet Shelter, along with the kids' sleeping bags and pillows.

"Don't forget the turtle!" yelled Zach, running to catch up.

7

The Sleepover

At first, Red and Lola seemed a little uneasy about having so many new neighbors in their barn. Red stamped his rear left hoof several times, and Lola stood as close to Red as she could get. But before long, all the animals settled down.

There were lots of things that needed to be done. First, the kids brought in all the supplies they'd gathered. They organized them neatly in a corner of the barn. Then they fed and watered all the animals. Lolli took care of the horses for Mrs. Jamison, since she was used to caring for larger animals. Adam, the expert dog walker, walked several dogs at once, including the big yellow Lab they'd seen from the bus, a pair of huskies, and Mr. and Mrs. Witherspoon's old dog, Rizzo. As the Pet Rescue Club had hoped, Mr. and Mrs. Witherspoon had agreed to go to the evacuation center at the high school once they knew that their dog would be cared for.

"I'm on turtle care!" said Zach, standing beside the glass box that contained the turtle. He reached into the box and petted the turtle's shell. "See? It's a lot of work!"

"You're kidding, right?" said Janey.

"Yeah, I guess he's pretty chill," Zach had to admit. "Or is he a she?"

Janey made comfortable dog and cat

beds from the moving blankets Mr. Teaberry had given them.

Then they all helped to put the pets in their beds for the night.

Mrs. Jamison was eager to use any food that might spoil in her refrigerator. She brought some frozen pizzas out to the barn and managed to cook them on the wood stove. As night fell, she lit glass hurricane lanterns.

"It's so cozy!" said Lolli, sitting on her unrolled sleeping bag. Everyone had brought sleeping bags and pillows to spend the night at the Big Red Pet Shelter.

Lolli's dad had offered to stay overnight in the barn. "I love a good campout," said Mr. Simpson. He had even brought a ukulele, and as it got close to bedtime, he sang songs

to comfort the restless animals, including "Old MacDonald Had a Farm," "Home on the Range," and "Whip-poor-will in the Canyon."

"Just another service of the Pet Rescue Club," said Zach. "Sing-along skills!"

Janey was quiet and happy. Earlier in the day, she had decided she couldn't leave little Disaster behind at the Third Street shelter. So she had taken the tiny puppy with her. Now she held Dizzy close. Soon Dizzy was fast asleep.

One by one, Lolli, Zach, and Adam fell asleep in their sleeping bags. Then Janey heard soft snores coming from across the barn where Mr. Simpson slept.

Only Janey stayed awake. She didn't want to miss a minute of this special time with Dizzy. She listened to the gentle snufflings and snorts of the sleeping animals all around. She fought to keep her eyes open for as long as she could.

But the next thing she knew, it was morning.

8

It's Raining Cats and Dogs

The next day dawned clear and sunny, and Janey woke up smiling. Disaster yawned. His little pink mouth and pointy teeth and sweet breath were right in Janey's face. Dizzy blinked. His brown eyes were alert and loving. She'd never been so happy in her life.

"Good morning, Dizzy," she whispered, stretching her legs to the bottom of her sleeping bag and wiggling her toes. The Big Red Pet Shelter was still quiet, though Janey could tell by gentle rustlings and quiet yips and soft meows that the pets were waking up all around the barn. Dizzy put out his little pink tongue and licked Janey's nose.

"Rise and shine!" came a singsong voice. It was Mrs. Jamison. "Good news," she said, as everyone stirred in their sleeping bags. "Watch this!" And she switched on the big overhead lights.

"The power's back on!" said Adam, sitting up.

"Finally, we can be normal and fire up the laptop," said Zach, breathing a sigh of relief. He really did not like to be far from a working computer at any time. "The past couple of days have been nuts."

"And that's not all. I have even more

good news," said Mrs. Jamison. "The sooner you get all these critters taken care of, the sooner you can come inside for a hot breakfast. Pancakes!"

Mr. Simpson was checking the chickens. He held up his findings in both hands. "And eggs!" he said.

Everyone cheered and got to work feeding and watering the pets. Once again, Adam took several dogs out at once. Zach took Rizzo and the two huskies, but he got their leashes all tangled up.

"Turtles are a lot easier to walk," Zach said, turning in circles to unwind a leash from his ankle.

While they ate the delicious breakfast Mrs. Jamison had made, Janey plugged in her laptop to charge. Then the Pet Rescue Club got back to work. This time, they used technology.

"Phew," said Zach. "The Internet service is back on!"

They went out to the barn and took a picture of each dog and cat, the guinea pigs, the chickens, the ferret, the corn snake, and the turtle. Then, back inside at Mrs. Jamison's kitchen table, they posted the pictures on their blog, Janey's Pet Place.

"Those are excellent photos," said Mrs. Jamison. "Every one of those pets could be a pet fashion model," she joked.

"Now we wait for the people to come and claim their pets," said Adam.

But there was one pet picture missing.

"Janey, what about Dizzy?" Lolli said. "His picture isn't here."

Janey shifted in her chair. "Oh, I guess I forgot," she said.

"You want Dizzy's person to find him, don't you?" Lolli asked. She shot a look at Janey. "Whoever it is must be worried sick!"

Zach held up the digital camera. "Smile and say kibble, Dizzy!" he said. Janey held Dizzy out so that Zach could take the picture.

Janey had not exactly "forgotten" to post a picture of the tiny puppy. She had to admit it. She would be happy if Dizzy's person never came to take him away.

Janey fought back tears as she posted the picture on the blog. She almost wished the photo wasn't so cute. With his now-bright eyes and that sweet, sweet face, Dizzy's person was sure to come running to claim him.

Janey wanted what was best for Dizzy. But she'd already started thinking of the little puppy as her own, somehow. Maybe what was best for Dizzy would be to live at the Third Street Animal Shelter forever and ever. There, she could visit him every day, just as if he really did belong to her. She closed the laptop. She felt guilty about it, but part of her hoped that Dizzy's person would never see that adorable picture.

....

A little later in the morning, Dr. Goldman visited the Big Red Pet Shelter to check on the pets there. She reported that people in town had begun to go back to their houses.

Huge, blue tarps covered up holes in roofs like the one at Adam's house. Workers had cleared away the worst of the debris. Phone and Internet services had been restored. Everyone was feeling like things were returning to normal.

Janey made another post on the blog to thank everyone, including business owners, like Ms. Winkins at the hardware store and Mr. Teaberry at the furniture shop, for their generous donations of supplies. Those same business owners put up signs in their stores to let the town know that people could be reunited with their pets at either the Third Street Animal Shelter or the Big Red Pet Shelter. Before noon, the first person found his way to Mrs. Jamison's barn.

"Hello, it's going to be a beautiful day in the valley today," said the man. He ran a hand over his smooth, close-cropped hair and smiled broadly with a lot of perfect white teeth.

Mrs. Jamison squinted at him. "Aren't you . . ." she began.

"Yes!" the man said. He stuck out his hand to shake Mrs. Jamison's. "Bob Broad, channel seven chief meteorologist. I lost my cat, Puddles, in the weather event."

Lolli invited Bob Broad into the barn to see if Puddles was there. Mr. Broad peered into each pet carrier and crate. In the very last one, there was a small gray kitty. "Puddles!" said Mr. Broad. He scooped the cat up in his arms. Puddles' purring could be heard all over the barn.

"How can I ever thank you for rescuing and sheltering my cat?" Mr. Broad asked, scratching Puddles behind the ears. She purred even louder. "I know!" he went on. "How about you kids come on the news tonight? All the world will know about your heroic efforts!" Mr. Broad grinned. "Well, the local broadcast area will, anyway. We'll tell people who are missing their pets to come and look for them here."

....

Janey could hardly believe it. Everyone's parents talked together and agreed to allow Janey, Lolli, Adam, and Zach appear on TV. That night on the six o'clock news, chief meteorologist Bob Broad made an announcement. "The tornado may be over, but at a

local pet shelter, it's raining cats and dogs! Isn't that right, Janey Whitfield?" he said, turning to Janey.

"Yes," said Janey, who had been elected by the Pet Rescue Club to speak for them. "Plus chickens, guinea pigs, a corn snake, and a ferret," she added. Zach jabbed her in the ribs. "And a turtle," she said.

Bob Broad faced the camera and smiled. "You heard it here, folks!" he declared. "If you and your pet have been separated, like me and my cat Puddles were, just look on the Janey's Pet Place blog to find out if your loved one is being cared for at the Pet Rescue Club's temporary shelter, the Big Red Pet Shelter! And please support your local pet shelter, the Third Street Animal Shelter. Give generously!"

And, because everyone in the local broadcast area had recently gotten back their electricity, people were so happy to be able to watch the news again. A record number of viewers had their television sets turned on that evening to see Bob Broad's piece about the Pet Rescue Club and the Big Red Pet Shelter.

9

Jojo!

The next day, people came to the barn bright and early.

The first one to arrive was the man Adam had met at the high school's evacuation center. When he caught sight of Adam, he waved.

"Hey, I saw you on TV last night," he said. "I said to myself, that's the boy I was telling about Jojo!" The man put his hands together as if he might be praying. "Please tell me Jojo's here," he said. "I've been sick about losing my best pal. When I saw you on

TV, that's when I started hoping again."

"Come in and have a look," said Adam. "I hope Jojo's here, too."

Inside the barn, Zach was getting ready to take the two huskies and the yellow Lab for a walk. He had the three dogs on leashes.

"Jojo!" the man cried when he spotted the big yellow Lab. He dropped to his knees and opened his arms wide. Jojo pulled on his leash, then suddenly broke free. Zach's feet went out from under him and he landed on the barn floor.

"Whoa!" Zach hollered. "You'd think he couldn't wait to get away from me," he muttered, as Adam took the huskies' leashes from him. "It's not like I've been taking care of that dog around the clock for two days straight or anything," he joked. "Ow," he said, rubbing an elbow where he'd fallen. "Dogs can be painfully loyal."

Meanwhile, Jojo ran into the man's arms so fast, he knocked him over. The man tumbled onto one side, laughing.

"It's like Jojo's bowling!" said Zach.

Zach and the man got to their feet and brushed themselves off. "Thank you for taking care of my best friend," the man said. "Jojo's collar had a tag with my name, address, and phone numbers on it. But the tag is missing. Somehow it must have gotten loose and came off." He bent and hugged Jojo again.

"It might be time to microchip Jojo," suggested Dr. Goldman. The vet had come to check on the animals, and also to check on Zach. "A microchip is as small as a grain of rice," she explained, "and it has an identification number on it. When you microchip your pet, you get the number and register your pet's name and your address and contact information with the microchip company. That way," she went on, "if a pet gets lost, when it's found, a quick scan of the chip will help reunite the pet with its owners. It's similar to scanning a grocery store item, but it's a different system."

"The chip always goes between the pet's shoulder blades," Zach chimed in. "That makes it easy to find and read. It's amazing technology. And the chip can't be lost, like a tag."

"All right, I'm sold," Jojo's person said

with a laugh. After gladly making a donation to the Third Street Animal Shelter, he and Jojo hopped into his car. He honked and waved as he drove away. Jojo stuck his head out the window to bark good-bye.

Soon a car with an elderly couple pulled up to the barn.

"Hello," said the man. "We are George and Martha Witherspoon, and we—"

"Rizzo!" Lolli broke in. "Sorry to interrupt," she said sheepishly.

Mr. and Mrs. Witherspoon's faces lit up. "Yes, that's right," said Mrs. Witherspoon, smiling. "Rizzo is our dog. May we see him?"

"Of course!" said Janey. She ran inside the barn and came back out with the old dog.

Rizzo knew better than to jump on his

elderly people, but he wagged his tail like crazy and smiled the way dogs do.

"Thank you for taking such good care of him," said Mr. Witherspoon. "I'm afraid we can't return to our house just yet. We only came out here for a visit. That is, we were hoping Rizzo could stay here for a few more days," Mr. Witherspoon said. He scratched Rizzo's back as he spoke, smiling all the while. Rizzo closed his eyes and leaned into Mr. Witherspoon's leg.

"Certainly," said Mrs. Jamison. "I'd be more than happy to keep Rizzo here for as long as you wish. He's an excellent guest, and he seems to get along very nicely with Red and Lola."

"That's very nice to hear," said Mrs. Witherspoon. "What kind of dogs are they?"

Everyone laughed.

"They're horses, actually," Mrs. Jamison explained.

Shortly after Mr. and Mrs. Witherspoon drove away, a woman and her sons came and claimed the pair of huskies. "They got out of the backyard when a tree fell on the fence and took it down," she said. Her two little boys buried their faces in the huskies' thick fur. "Everything happened pretty fast," she said, shaking her head. "I was at work, and the boys were with my mother. I just couldn't make it home in time." She watched her little boys playing with the dogs, a small smile on her face. "Thank you," she said quietly. "I'm very grateful."

In the next few hours, all the cats were claimed. Someone came looking for Mango the snake. The ferret belonged to a tall, skinny man named Bert. Mrs. Brick collected her chickens. By the end of the day only Rizzo, the guinea pigs, the turtle, and a puppy called Disaster remained.

10

Dizzy

Several more days passed. The landlord patched the roof of Adam's house. He and his parents and sister moved back home.

"Too bad you can't see the stars from your bed anymore," said Zach. "That was cool."

Almost all the shelter pets had been claimed. The guinea pigs' person had turned out to be a woman who had a twin sister. She said she had always had pets in pairs.

And school had started up again. The four members of the Pet Rescue Club were seated in the cafeteria, having a lunchtime meeting.

Janey had another large cookie. She divided it and handed out the pieces to her friends.

"Oh, great," said Zach, eyeing the cookie wrapper and the dome-shaped, pink coconut cookie. "This one's called a Snowball. We're probably in for a blizzard."

Janey saved the banana part of her lunch for later. The Third Street Animal Shelter was only a few blocks from school, and Janey's parents had given her permission to walk straight there each day after school. She often got hungry late in the afternoon, and she liked to have a snack.

Janey bit into her cookie. She knew she should care that nobody had come looking for Dizzy. She knew that someone must be missing that little pup. But that person could not love Dizzy more than Janey did. It had been wonderful to be able to visit the puppy every day after school now that he and the turtle had been moved from the Big Red Pet Shelter to the Third Street shelter. It was almost like having a puppy of her own.

Every day, she helped Kitty for a while and then played with Dizzy and held him. Sometimes she even did her homework at the shelter. That way, she could stay longer with "her" dog.

"Maybe no one will ever come to claim him," she said to her friends. "Maybe he can live at the Third Street Animal Shelter forever." She doodled a tiny puppy on her paper napkin. "That way he would sort of belong to me."

Lolli and Adam shared a worried look.

"Maybe," said Lolli, doubtfully.

"You can always hope," said Adam.

"Fat chance," said Zach.

Janey ignored them all.

....

A couple of days later, a young woman came into the Third Street Animal Shelter. Lolli, Adam, and Zach had walked with Janey to the shelter after school. Janey had just put Dizzy into his cozy little crate in the dog room. It was almost time to go home.

"How can we help you?" asked Kitty.

The woman looked sad. Her eyes were red-rimmed. "I guess I'd like to adopt a dog," she said. She took a tissue from her bag and blew her nose. "Is it too late to do that today?"

"Not at all," Kitty said. "Please sit down, and we'll talk." Kitty led the woman into the Meet-and-Greet room. "I'm Kitty, and these are my Pet Rescue Club friends. They've been helping me count my supplies and make a list of what we need."

The woman's name was Deb. "I lost my puppy in the tornado," Deb said. She tore the tissue apart with anxious fingers.

"Oh, that's terrible," said Kitty. "I am sorry for your loss."

"Thank you." Deb shook her head. "I had seen this puppy in the shelter in the town where I used to live and couldn't resist him, even though I was about to move here. Then I moved here just two days before the tornado. A new puppy and a new house would have been more than enough for me," said Deb, gulping in air. "Then the tornado hit and the puppy disappeared. I didn't know the first thing about where to look. I've stayed home, hoping against hope that he'd somehow find his way back there. But he was such a tiny little guy. I hadn't even named him yet!"

"That's very sad," Lolli said. She glanced at Janey. "Do you mind if I ask what kind of dog he was?"

Janey had a bad feeling in the pit of her stomach. She wondered if there was such a thing as an anxiety vest for people. "Maybe Deb doesn't want to talk about it," she blurted out. "Maybe it's too painful for her."

Kitty patted Deb's hands. "We are here to listen, if you want to talk."

Deb's eyes teared up, and she dabbed at them with the crumpled bits of tissue. "He wasn't any particular breed," she said. "But he looked like he had a lot of beagle in him."

There was a silent moment. Janey and Lolli and Adam and Zach and Kitty all looked at each other.

"What is it?" Deb asked. "Did I say something wrong?"

Then everyone started smiling and talking at once.

"What's going on?" asked Deb.

"Deb, I think we have wonderful news for you," Kitty said. She turned to Janey and put a gentle hand on her arm. "Janey, do you want to go and get someone from his crate?" she asked.

"Not really," Janey said. She looked at Deb, and then at her feet. "But I will."

Janey went into the dog room and took Dizzy out of his crate. The puppy licked her cheek, and she held him close. She could feel his little heart beating. "I guess this is good-bye," she whispered. "I love you, Dizzy." She gave Dizzy one more kiss on the top of his head. Then she went back into the Meet-and-Greet room.

"It's him!" Deb said to Kitty. "It's you!" she said to the puppy, holding her hands out to take him from Janey. "I've been so worried," she said. "I'd given up hope I'd ever see him again!"

Kitty explained how Mr. Petersen had brought the puppy to the shelter the day after

the tornado. She told Deb how the Pet Rescue Club had taken good care of the puppy. "But it was Janey who took special care of him," Kitty said. "Almost as if he was her own."

Deb looked around at everyone one by one. "How can I ever thank you enough for saving my little lost puppy? Especially you,

Janey. Thank you. Oh, Rover!" she cried, hugging the puppy.

Rover? Zach mouthed.

"Or do you look more like a Charlie?" Deb asked. She tipped her head and peered into the puppy's bright, shining eyes. "Peanut?" She shrugged. "I still haven't decided on the perfect name for my perfect puppy." She tucked the little dog under her chin, closed her eyes, and smiled blissfully.

Janey cleared her throat. "We've been calling him Dizzy, short for Disaster."

Deb's eyes snapped open. "Disaster," she said. "Disaster?" She held the little dog out in front of her and they rubbed noses. "Perfect," she said. "Hello, Disaster. Hello, Dizzy."

Deb thanked the Pet Rescue Club again

for saving her puppy and for giving him the perfect name. "You are all welcome to visit anytime. My house is just a few blocks from the school." Before leaving the shelter, Deb even signed up with Adam for future dog walking and training sessions. Then Deb and Dizzy walked out the door.

Janey watched them go. She held back her tears, and she really was happy for Deb and for Dizzy.

"Cheer up, Janey," said Zach, reaching into a glass box. "There's this nice turtle nobody has come to claim . . . your dad wouldn't be allergic to a cute, cuddly turtle, would he?"

Even Janey had to laugh.

The very next day, Lolli and Janey went to visit Dizzy at Deb's house. And Lolli had an idea. "The Pet Rescue Club should do something before the next disaster strikes," Lolli said. "Remember that emergency preparedness class the Red Cross gave the town? We should organize a class that's all about pet care during an emergency!"

"Prodigious!" said Janey. She held Dizzy and kissed his little nose. "And I think we have the perfect pet-preparedness mascot," she said. "A puppy called Disaster!"

Are You Ready?

You can put together your own basic emergency kit for your pets. Keep your pets' supplies in a sturdy container that can be easily carried, like a duffel bag or a trash bin with a lid. Your pet emergency preparedness kit should include:

✓ Current photos of you with your pet in case your pet gets lost.

✓ Your pet's medications and medical records (stored in a waterproof container) and a first aid kit.

✓ Sturdy leashes, harnesses, and/or carriers to transport animals safely and ensure your pet can't escape.

✓ Food, drinkable water, bowls, cat litter and pan, and manual can opener.

✓ Garbage bags to collect your pet's waste.

✓ Information on feeding schedules, medical conditions, behavior problems, and the name and number of your vet.

✓ Pet bed or toys if easily transportable.

✓ The ASPCA recommends using a rescue alert sticker to let people know that pets are inside your home. Make sure it is visible to rescue workers, and that it includes the types and number of pets in your household, as well as your veterinarian's phone number. If you evacuate with your pets, write"EVACUATED" across the sticker, if you can, so rescue workers don't waste valuable time looking for them.

REMEMBER!

If it's not safe for you, it's not safe for your pets!

A Real Disaster

Hurricane Katrina hit southeast Louisiana on August 29, 2005. It became one of the deadliest storms to ever hit the United States. Hundreds of thousands of people and their pets were affected. Animal rescue groups, including the ASPCA, rushed to the scene as soon as they could to help save lives and reunite people with pets.

After the storm, it became apparent that the needs of pets should be part of disaster planning. Acts were passed in Congress that

added pets to federal guidelines. According to the ASPCA, these laws not only save lives, but they elevate the issue of animal safety to its rightful place among other natural disaster priorities.

Have you read the other PET RESCUE CLUB Chapter Books?

In case you missed it, here are some pages from, Book #2: No Time for Hallie.

1

Bird Alert

"Good kitty, Mulberry." Janey Whitfield patted the fat orange tabby cat that had just jumped onto the sofa beside her. She giggled as he rubbed his face on her arm. "Your whiskers tickle! Aw, but that's okay—you love me, don't you?"

"He's just hoping you'll give him more food," Zach Goldman said with a laugh.

Mulberry was Zach's family's cat. Janey was at Zach's house, along with their friends Lolli Simpson and Adam Santos. Today was the first official meeting of the Pet Rescue Club—the group the four of them had decided to form after helping to rescue a neglected dog.

The meeting had started half an hour earlier. Zach's dad had brought out some snacks, and the four kids were supposed to be discussing how to organize their new group. But, they'd been too busy eating and playing with Mulberry to do much discussing so far.

Lolli selected a piece of cheese off the tray on the coffee table. "Did you add the stuff about the Pet Rescue Club to the blog?" she asked Janey.

"Yes." Janey pushed Mulberry away gently. Then she picked up her tablet computer and showed Lolli the screen.

Janey's blog had started as a way for kids around their town to share photos of their pets. Janey loved animals, but she couldn't have a pet of her own because her father was severely allergic to anything with fur or feathers. She'd thought that seeing pictures of lots of cute pets would be the next best thing to having her own.

Now the blog had another purpose, too. The Pet Rescue Club was going to use it to find animals that needed their help. So far, Janey had written an update on the rescued dog and added a paragraph telling people to send in information on any animal that might need their help.

"Okay," Adam said. "So we put something on the blog. Now what?"

Adam was a very practical person. He was so responsible that he already had a successful pet-sitting business, even though he was only nine. People all over town paid him to come to their houses to feed and walk their dogs while they were at work or on vacation.

Janey didn't answer Adam right away. Mulberry was kneading his front paws on her leg and purring. Janey rubbed the cat's head and smiled.

"I wish I could have a cat like Mulberry," she said.

"Yeah, Mulberry is great!" Lolli leaned over to pet the cat. Mulberry turned around and butted his head against her arm.

Janey giggled. "And he's so cute! Here, Mulberry—want a cracker?"

"Don't give him that," Zach said quickly. "It's onion flavored and cats shouldn't eat onion—it's bad for them."

"Really?" Janey wasn't sure whether to believe him. Zach was always joking around and playing pranks on people. Still, she didn't want to hurt Mulberry if Zach was being serious for once. She pulled the cracker away and glanced at Adam. "Is that true? Are onions bad for cats?"

Adam shrugged. "Probably. I know dogs aren't supposed to eat onions."

"Why are you asking him? Don't you believe me?" Zach asked Janey. "My mom's a vet, you know. She's taught me lots of stuff like that."

Before Janey could answer, a pair of

twelve-year-old boys raced into the room. They were identical twins. Both of them were tall and skinny with wavy dark hair and the same brown eyes as Zach. It was raining outside, and the boys' sneakers left wet tracks on the floor.

Janey knew the twins were two of Zach's three older brothers. She couldn't imagine living with that many boys!

"Check it out," one of the twins said, pointing at Janey. "Little Zachie has a girlfriend!"

"No way—he has two girlfriends! Way to go, little bro!" the other boy exclaimed with a grin.

"Shut up!" Zach scowled at them. "And go away. We're trying to have a meeting here."

One of the twins stepped over and grabbed Mulberry off the sofa. "Yo, Mulberry," he said, cuddling the cat. "Are these girls bothering you?"

"Mulberry likes us," Lolli said with

a smile. "He's like the mascot of the Pet Rescue Club."

"Okay." The twin dropped Mulberry on the sofa again. The cat sat down and started washing his paw.

"Grab the umbrella and let's go," the other twin said. "The guys are waiting for us outside."

One of the twins grabbed an umbrella off a hook by the back door. Then they raced back out of the room.

"Sorry about that," Zach muttered. "They are so annoying."

"They're not so bad." Lolli smiled. She got along with everybody—even obnoxious boys. "Anyway, what were we talking about?"

"About how cats can't eat onion," Zach

said. "They shouldn't have chocolate, either. Did you know that?" He stared at Janey.

She shrugged. "No. That's interesting."

"Yeah," Lolli agreed. "There's lots to know about having a pet! When we first got Roscoe, I thought all he needed was a bowl of water and some dog food. But there's a lot more to it than that!"

Roscoe was the Simpsons' big, lovable dog. Lolli and her parents had found him at the Third Street Animal Shelter a few years earlier. He was a mix of Labrador retriever, rottweiler, and who knew what else.

"I have an idea," Janey said. "You already said Mulberry was our club mascot. We should make Roscoe a mascot, too. We can post their pictures on the blog to make it official."

"Good idea," Lolli said. "I have a cute picture of Roscoe we can use."

"We should take a picture of Mulberry riding on my skateboard," Zach said. "That would be cool!"

"Veto," Janey replied.

Zach frowned at her. "Can't you just say no like a normal person?" he said. "Oh, wait, I forgot—you're not normal."

Janey ignored him. "Veto" was her new favorite word. Janey liked finding interesting words and using them. Saying veto was her new way of saying no.

"Hey Janey," Adam spoke up. "I think I heard your tablet ping."

"Really?" Janey had dropped her tablet

on the sofa. Now Mulberry was sitting on it. She pulled the tablet out from under the cat. "Sorry, Mulberry. That might be an animal who needs our help!"

Lolli leaned over her shoulder. "What does it say?"

"It's not a posting on the blog," Janey said. "It's alerting me to a new e-mail."

She clicked into her e-mail account. The message was from a classmate named Leah. Janey read it quickly.

Hi Janey,

I heard you're helping animals now. I need help! I just got home from my soccer practice and found out my pet canary is missing!

2

Runaway Cat?

"Oh, no!" Janey exclaimed, reading the e-mail again.

"What's wrong?" Adam asked.

"The e-mail is from Leah," Janey said. "She says her canary is missing!"

"Leah has a canary?" Lolli said. "I didn't know that."

"I didn't either. But if it's missing, we should try to help her find it," Janey said. "Zach, may I use the phone?"

"Sure, that'll be five dollars, please," Zach said.

Janey ignored the joke. She rushed into

the kitchen and grabbed the phone. Leah had put her number at the end of the e-mail.

"Janey?" Leah said from the other end of the line. "I was hoping you'd call. I'm so worried about Sunny!"

"What happened?" Janey asked.

"I must have forgotten to latch his cage after I fed him this morning before school." Leah sounded upset. "When I got home, the cage door was open and Sunny was nowhere in sight!"

"Oh, no," Janey exclaimed.

"That's not even the worst part," Leah went on. "My bedroom window was open! What if he flew outside? I might never find him!"

Janey glanced at Lolli, Adam, and Zach. They had followed her into the kitchen and were all listening to her half of the conversation.

"Don't worry, Leah," Janey said. "The Pet Rescue Club is on it! We'll be right over."

She hung up and told the others what Leah had said. "I don't like the idea of keeping birds cooped up in cages," Lolli said uncertainly. "Shouldn't they be free to fly around?"

"I don't know," Janey said. "But Leah sounded really worried."

"Then we should help her," Lolli said.

Here are all the other books in the
PET RESCUE CLUB
series!

 1 A New Home for Truman

Janey can't have a pet of her own because of her father's allergies. Her love for animals is so strong, though, that it leads her and her friends to create the Pet Rescue Club to help animals in need, like Truman the dog!

 2 No Time for Hallie

Can the Pet Rescue Club help a senior cat find a new home when her owners decide they no longer have the time or attention to give her?

 3 The Lonely Pony

When Adam finds Lola, a neglected pony, the Pet Rescue Club is determined to find her a better home, despite the challenges of caring properly for a small horse.

 4 Too Big to Run

Maxi runs with her owner who is training for a marathon, but all that running is not good for Maxi's knees. When she winds up needing an operation, the Pet Rescue Club raises the money to pay for the surgery, and then gets Maxi a new job!